# 丁仔
# 去露營
## Js go camping

作者／文與清

繪畫／小羊

寶藏──藏於簡單的真實故事中……
Something priceless to be unlocked in a simple story based on real-life experience!

菜頭一直夢想長大後成為領袖。

Tsoi aspires to be a leader when he grows up.

菜頭有一羣好朋友，經常出外活動。

He has a group of good friends.
They enjoy going on outdoor activities very much.

因年紀很輕，別人都稱他們做「J」仔。

Being juniors, they are nicknamed as "J Chai"!

夏日露營！！

Summer Camp!!

每人都有自己最棒的地方，各展所長。
菜頭沒有特別技能，但知道怎樣去協助完成工作，
大家有時會忽略了他。

Every time Js work as a team, each doing what he does best. Tsoi does not have a special talent, but he is apt at helping others complete their tasks. Sometimes though, the others might forget he's around!

他們最喜歡就是夜行……
卻是不帶電筒！

Their favourite activity is
Night March......
without a torch!

眼睛會適應環境⋯⋯
Eyes will adapt......

行、行、行……
不知誰踢到了 蜂巢！！

On they marched, till someone kicked a hive!!

蜂巢保衛戰！
有敵人來襲！
衝！衝！衝！

Mission Hive Defence!!!!
Enemies are approaching!

Attack!

J仔們奮力頑抗！

J Chai fought back with all their strength!

忽然有人高聲呼喊：「伏低啊！」

Suddenly, someone shouted "Lie Prone!"

大家都受了傷…呀！……呀！

Everyone got stung ... yikes! ...... ouch!

菜頭傷勢不重，他立即拿出帶備了的藥物、繃帶，

還有……　電筒！

Tsoi was relatively unscathed. He immediately
searched his rucksack: first aid medicine,

bandages and ...... torch!

他們彼此扶持，走向安全地方，並通知救援到來，
全隊也獲得了很多經驗！

他們已經準備另一次的歷險……

They supported each other and headed to a safe
spot where they could wait for rescue. The whole
team gained a lot of valuable experience!

They are ready for another adventure ......

追隨自己那

心中的小孩

Follow our

inner child

書法／Jt 與 Js
菜頭＆菜婆的外甥孫

# 如何發掘領袖才能?

這是一本鼓勵親子閱讀的圖書,在大家閱讀的時間,也不妨參考一下作者提議的幾個與孩子一起思考的地方。

- 菜頭只是故事橋段的主線,他可以不是主角,讀者們可以與家人嘗試另找一位在故事中的 J 仔,然後以他的第一身,再講述同樣的故事,看看有沒有新的發現?! 當你細看畫中不同的 J 仔造型、表情及動作,或許會給你不少啓發。

- 除 J 仔外,有留意到別的角色嗎?牠們的生態,有沒有令你同時聯想起一些領袖才能?

- 領袖才能不止於概念上的東西,讀者與家人可以談談如何能將才能活現出來,例如勇敢怎樣應用到生活上?

- J 仔全隊不止發揮他們的領袖才能,還看到自己的缺點,因為他們心裏明白人的優劣個性是互相關連,知優明劣,方能成為好領袖。

- 讀者們,你們又有沒有留意故事中 J 仔們的缺點呢?

## How to Unlock the Leadership within ?

This storybook aims to encourage family reading. During the course of your reading, the following points might be worth discussing:

Tsoi is one of the main characters of this story, but he does not necessarily have to be the leading character. Readers can choose their own favourite J Chai, tell the story from his point of view and see if anything new can be discovered. Look closely at each of the J Chai, examine their expressions and their actions, and you might get new inspirations!

Apart from J Chai, pay attention to the other characters. Can you identify any leadership skills from their behaviour?

Leadership is not merely a theoretical concept. Try discussing with your family how to put leadership skills, e.g. bravery, into practice.

J Chai didn't just demonstrate leadership skills, they were also aware of their shortcomings. In fact, to be a good leader, one needs to understand one's strengths and weaknesses. Dear readers, can you point out the shortcomings of J Chai?

繪畫：中譚的兒子

　　從經歷中，J 仔們總共運用了至少 12 項領袖才能！你看到嗎？試想你與家人遇到危險，你又可以有哪些領袖才能用得着呢？

- During their experience, J Chai demonstrated at least 12 types of leadership skills. Can you identify them?

- If you are in danger, which of your leadership skills might be of use?

如對此書有任何回應或心事分享，請電郵至 tsoimc@alumni.cuhk.net

We would love to hear your feedback of our story!

Please email to tsoimc@alumni.cuhk.net

想一想，這些都是50年前的事了……

在記憶中，以前香港有過一隊陸軍軍團，設立過一團的少年中隊，他們是同輩中的精英，而並非如現在某些香港掌故中記述，他們是失學兒童！

我並沒有成為甚麼出名的領袖，一生只是好好的照顧家人，退休，結婚，從生活中鍛鍊出來的領袖能力，幫助了我快樂地生活，無論何時何地，我知道它也會用得上！

菜頭
2020

YO. 2020. 31·10

All these happened 50 years ago ...

As I remember, there was really a cadet squadron affiliated to a regiment in Hong Kong. Its members were among the elites of their generation, in contrast to what has been claimed by some reports.

I did not grow up to be a famous leader. Throughout my life, I have strived to look after my family and to do my best, in work and in life. Retired and married, the leadership skills that I have accumulated over the years have enabled me to enjoy a happy and fulfilled life. I know that these skills will come in handy anywhere, anytime!

TSOI
2020

# 鳴謝篇

- 多謝繪畫的小羊，不眠不休地工作，多謝、多謝！
- 多謝參與繪畫的小朋友、中譚和文 Sir 拔刀相助，多謝、多謝！
- 多謝寫字的小朋友，平日古靈精「靈」，原來咁好書法，多謝、多謝！
- 多謝紅出版，一別 12 年，幹勁勝以前，多謝、多謝！
- 多謝讀者，沒有讀者，作家哪來收入，多謝、多謝！

# Acknowledgements

- Special thanks to Sheep Young, for working and drawing 24/7!
- Many thanks to Tam, Man Sir and our little artists for volunteering to help!
- Many thanks to our young calligraphers, didn't realise their hidden penmanship!
- Many thanks to Red Publish. It is great to see you grow in strength since our last collaboration 12 years ago!
- Many thanks to our readers for buying our book!

題目：兩隻企鵝
攝影：菜婆 & 菜頭
地點：南極
活動：camping
日期：X'mas 2015

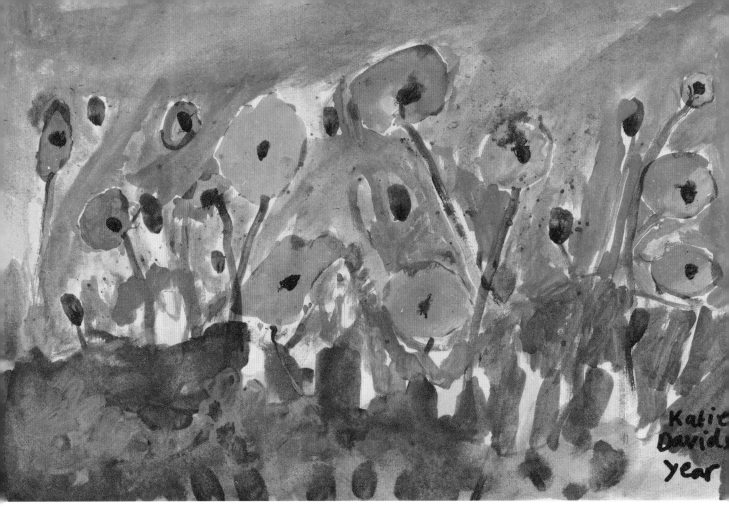

繪畫：文 Sir 的外孫女

作者：文與清
封面、封底及內文插畫：小羊 (sheepsheep12@gmail.com)
設計：4res
編輯：Nancy

紅出版（青森文化）
地址：香港灣仔道一三三號卓凌中心十一樓
出版計劃查詢電話：(852) 2540 7517
電郵：editor@red-publish.com
網址：http://www.red-publish.com

香港總經銷：香港聯合書刊物流有限公司
　　　　　　香港新界大埔汀麗路 36 號中華商務印刷大廈三字樓
台灣總經銷：貿騰發賣股份有限公司
　　　　　　新北市中和區中正路 880 號 14 樓
　　　　　　(886) 2-8227-5988
　　　　　　http://www.namode.com

出版日期：二零二零年十二月
圖書分類：兒童讀物
國際標準書號：978-988-8743-00-1
定價：港幣八十元正 / 新台幣三百二十圓正